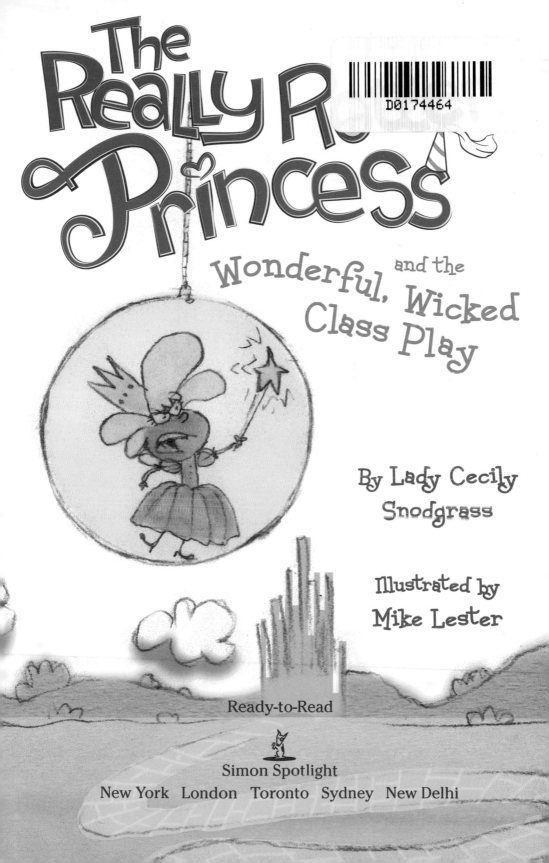

The Really Rotten Princess

Wonderful, and the Wicked Class Play

By Lady Cecily
Snodgrass

Illustrated by
Mike Lester

Ready-to-Read

Simon Spotlight

New York   London   Toronto   Sydney   New Delhi

SIMON SPOTLIGHT
An imprint of Simon & Schuster Children's Publishing Division
1230 Avenue of the Americas, New York, New York 10020
This Simon Spotlight edition August 2022
Copyright © 2022 by Simon & Schuster, Inc.

SIMON SPOTLIGHT, READY-TO-READ, and colophon are registered trademarks of Simon & Schuster, Inc.
For information about special discounts for bulk purchases, please contact Simon & Schuster Special Sales at 1-866-506-1949 or business@simonandschuster.com.
Manufactured in the United States of America 0722 LAK
10 9 8 7 6 5 4 3 2 1
ISBN 978-1-5344-8618-8 (hc)
ISBN 978-1-5344-8617-1 (pbk)
ISBN 978-1-5344-8619-5 (ebook)
Library of Congress Catalog Card Number 2022935306

Chapter One

Once she realized
the role came with no real power,
Regina quit her job as class
president . . .

. . . much to the relief
of her classmates.

So she decided she needed to find
a new way to annoy them.

When Miss Prunerot announced that tryouts would be held for a class play, Regina saw her chance.

Each princess had an idea as to which play the class should put on.

But Regina beat them to the punch . . .

Chapter Two

Miss Prunerot announced the play that the class would be performing.

The first job was to cast the show. Princess Dragonbreath was chosen to play Dorothy.

The parts of the Scarecrow, the Tin Man, and the Cowardly Lion went to Princesses Litterati, Glitterati, and Lovelylocks.

And the role of the Wizard
went to Princess Wishlicious.

That left just two key parts to fill.

In the end Miss Prunerot made the decision.

REGINA WILL PLAY GLINDA . . . THE GOOD.

THAT'S CALLED CASTING AGAINST TYPE.

And she named Princess Seafoam as the director of the play.

THNKS A LT.

The entire castle was thrilled to see Regina home for the long weekend . . .

. . . especially the court wizard, Maldemar.

Without even knowing it, he gave her a wonderfully rotten idea.

So just before leaving
to return to school,
Regina borrowed
something from him.

Chapter Three

Back at school, rehearsals were going much better.

JUST TAP YOUR SHOES AND SAY, "THERE'S NO PLACE LIKE HOME."

VERY GOOD, REGINA!

SH'S UP T SMTHNG.

And at the end of the week,
the princesses' parents arrived
for the performance.

The show started out okay.
At least until Dorothy got to Oz.
Then Regina came on stage.

But Regina wasn't done yet. She turned Princess Lovelylocks into a real lion.

IS THERE SOMETHING DIFFERENT ABOUT ME?

And then . . .

LET'S SEE HOW ALL OF YOU LIKE BEING STUCK IN BUBBLES.

Until Maldemar took back
what was rightfully his . . .

I BELIEVE
THIS IS MINE.

. . . and gave Regina the punishment she deserved.

WELL, YOU DID WANT TO BE THE WICKED WITCH.